THE MOST CURIOUS CASE

A Rex Haining Mystery

Jason Fischer

Cayuga Publishing LLC

Cover design by: Val Fischer Art

Printed in the United States of America

CONTENTS

THE MOST CURIOUS CASE

THE MURDER

Fumbling with her keys, Helen Jackson struggled to open the locked door to her office in the mayor's mansion. Once open, she wondered why Mr. Gavin, the personal secretary to the visiting president of Sri Lanka, hadn't turned on a single light. It was remarkably dark for this time of day, as heavy rain had been pummeling the city for the past two hours, obscuring the dwindling daylight. Wondering why anyone would be sitting alone in such a dark room, her question was answered when she inadvertently kicked the body lying on the floor.

Gasping at the sight, she fought to regain her balance, flinging her arms out. Nearly straddling him, she looked at the dead man. Mr. Gavin's hand was resting on his chest, where he wore an orchid. In the shadows of the room, her eyes darted around, trying to make sense of what she was encountering. Her heart beating rapidly, words came out in a jumbled stutter: "Sir, are...you...all right?"

Her question was met with silence. With the tip of her shoe, she lightly tapped his shoulder. His hand rolled off his chest, revealing a tear in his shirt. Between the white fibers was his exposed chest, revealing a small wound with a stream of blood trailing from it. With her stomach knotting up, she kneeled beside him, her knee instantly wet from the pooled blood.

With fingers shaking, she placed her hand on his neck. His flesh was as cold as ice. Jerking her hand away as if she had encountered something poisonous, she screamed, "Help!"

As she stood up, she was almost knocked over when Alfred Winnipeg burst through the door, bumping into her. His hand was gripping the butt of the revolver protruding from his waistband.

Helen stepped back, her bottom bumping into her desk behind her. The large man swiftly bent down and pulled back Mr. Gavin's sleeve. She maneuvered herself to the right so that she could better observe what Mr. Winnipeg was doing. He wrapped his enormous hands around Mr. Gavin's wrist.

In a trembling voice, Helen asked the questions she already knew the answer to. "Is he... dead?"

"Don't know for sure, but I think so." With his thumb and forefinger, he grabbed the lapel beside the entry wound and pulled at the flower. He plucked a few petals and held them under the man's nose, leaning in close. Shaking his head, he stood up.

Mr. Winnipeg reeked of tobacco, mixed with the smell of dampness that was always present in the room. Helen recoiled, trying to avoid contact. She had never seen a dead body before. Her mother didn't believe in children going to funerals, and Helen adhered to her wishes over the years, eventually developing a phobia that she never challenged—even when she had a choice. Now, forced to confront the fear with a relative stranger, her fingers kept shaking. In a whisper, she asked, "How did this happen?"

The officer opened his mouth to answer when Mayor Hitch entered the office and loudly asked, "What's the meaning of this?"

Before anyone could answer, the mayor stopped dead in his tracks. The self-assured look that got him reelected multiple times disappeared as he said, "What's going on here?" Adjusting his glasses, he barked, "Ms. Jackson, turn the lights on immediately!"

The command steadied her nerves, giving her something useful to do. Moving like an animal on a leash in a silent, obedient stride, she walked behind the desk. Once light filled the room, Mr. Hitch looked at the floor, staring at the corpse.

He said in a near whisper, "Oh, no." The second the words were spoken, he looked at Helen as though it were the first time he realized he wasn't alone in the room. A flash of recognition disappeared as his eyes narrowed.

Winnipeg mumbled into a mic near his wrist. His determined stare never left, even as he glared at the dead man. Looking back into the waiting room just outside the office that was used by the mayor's wife, he walked to the door—with a smooth, efficient stride—and slammed it shut. Helen couldn't see his hands, but she heard the familiar click of the key in the door.

"Sir, please move to that corner, out of view of the window." He pointed with one hand and pulled his gun free of the holster with the other, his eyes scanning the room the entire time. The mayor, taking a quick step back, stood against the wall, and Helen joined him.

Swiftly, Winnipeg moved to the window. Pulling his sleeve over his hand, he shook the latch, confirming it was secure. He then bent down, placing his hand on the wood floor and swiping at it. She assumed he was checking whether the floor was dry, as if someone could climb that easily into the mansion's third-story window.

Pulling the drapes shut on all four windows, Mr. Winnipeg strode across the room, carefully avoiding the dead body. He bent and looked beneath Ms. Jackson's desk, craning his head back to avoid a hidden attack from an unseen enemy. Straightening up with an earnest look, he said as much to himself as to the room, "Nothing here." The comment was received with a collective sigh of relief. His face was red from the slight exertion as he jammed the gun back into the holster.

Helen, thinking the killer could somehow still be hiding, turned her attention to the curtains, noting whether they were flat against the wall. Her eyes slowly swept the room. She looked past her and the mayor's wife's desks, which were parallel to the window wall, then to the opposite side of the room, which was large enough to hold 40 visitors. The wall had tiered shelving, like a miniature grandstand, from floor to ceiling, filled with collectibles from various visiting dignitaries. Glancing at the dolls, decorative ornaments, and ancient coins, she knew there was nowhere to hide among the items, yet it didn't lessen her fear.

There was a heavy knock at the door. Winnipeg placed his hand to his ear and spoke into his wrist. "Hang on." He unlocked the door, saying, "The room is clear."

Four men entered the space, all having wires in their ears, like Winnipeg. The tallest of the group, wearing a wrinkled suit, asked, "Mr. Hitch, are you all right?"

"Yes, Tom." The mayor's eyes never left the man on the floor as his foot nervously tapped the aged hardwood.

Tom switched his gaze to Winnipeg. "Alfie, what happened?"

"Sir, you ain't going to believe this." He looked up from the tablet he was holding. "Cameras and alarms show that neither the windows nor the doors have been opened in the last hour when I saw him enter the room."

The mayor interrupted, "Is *he* one of your men?"

"Sir, the deceased is Raymond Gavin. He's your guest's, well, I guess you could call him a bodyguard. You met him earlier."

"Oh, I can't see his face from here. Of course, I remember him now."

"Looks like he was stabbed."

The mayor responded, "Well, that's fantastic."

For a brief second, Tom's shoulders slumped as he let out a deep sigh. Quickly, as though a veil had been pulled over his face, the head of the mayor's security looked like a statue once again as he asked, "You've been outside the door since he entered this room, Winnipeg?"

"Yeah."

"And nobody's come in?"

"Other than Miss Jackson a minute ago, correct." He blinked twice, then held up the tablet with recognition coming to his expression. "Look, this confirms it, boss."

The mayor asked forcefully, "Then how did he end up stabbed?"

Winnipeg rubbed at the beginnings of beard stubble. "Don't know. Maybe he tripped and fell onto...whatever impaled him."

Tom knelt carefully next to the dead man. "Then where's the weapon?"

Winnipeg grunted out, "Yeah, good point."

Tom's intense gaze went to Helen. "How long were you here with him alone, Helen?"

"Not more than a few seconds, sir." Realizing what the head of the mayor's security detail was hinting at, Helen's heart skipped a beat. She wished that she'd headed home early, as originally planned, instead of coming back to the office.

INVESTIGATION HOUR ONE

Rex stared out the window, making a silent bet with himself that the golfer in the obnoxious pants was going to miss the fairway that surrounded the townhouse he had been staying in rent-free. Over the past few months, living so near the fourth tee, he was getting very good at guessing. His hypothesis was based on the expense of the clubs. The guys with the most expensive sets always seemed to be the worst golfers. He considered recording his findings, but doing so would force him to admit how bored he was becoming while not working.

The phone rang. Seeing it was Charles, he reluctantly hit the talk button. He was bored, but not so bored that he was unwilling to get to work. "To what do I owe this great honor?"

"I need you to get downtown."

"I'm doing well. Thanks for asking."

"No time for clowning here, bud."

The golfer finally made contact, and the ball went straight into the rough. Rex gave a quick fist pump, cheering silently. "That serious, huh?"

"Yeah. You're not going to like this, friend, but I need you to do it."

Turning on the sarcasm for his ex-partner, he

said, "I got a busy evening ahead of me." He glanced longingly at the paperback and the bag of open Fritos on the table next to a very comfortable couch that served as Rex's bed more nights than not. There was a perfectly good bed in the master bedroom, but whenever he slept in it, his mind would wander too much, questioning how long he was going to keep hiding out in the suburbs. "What happens if I say no?"

"For starters, you can start paying me the back rent." Then Rex heard some shuffling of papers. "Last time I checked, you're about a half year behind now."

"Hey, no reason to get nasty. I was speaking only hypothetically." He sat up and ran his hand through his hair, trying to remember the last time he had taken a shower. Giving up, he finally gave the lawyer, who was like a brother, his full attention. "So, what's the deal?"

"Before you interrupt, remember you're doing this because I need you to—agreed?"

Rex knew this one was going to hurt. Whenever Charles pulled the buddy card, it did. He knew he had no real choice, and even if he did, he'd do whatever he could. "All right, I'm all in. Now, the suspense is killing me. What's going on?"

"Well, we got a bit of a locked-room mystery here, and I'm going to need your skills to solve it."

"Sounds intriguing."

"Yeah, it really is. Beyond the circumstances, Rex…it's at the mayor's residence."

Rex tensed up, the stress settling in his neck. "I think we have a bad connection, but I believe you just said the *mayor's house*?"

"No, you heard me right."

"The same man who approved clipping me and putting me on a partial pension?"

"Look, I get it, but remember—you told me you were in."

"Chuck, come on!" He rubbed the back of his neck. His index finger rested on a scar that ran the width of his neck. He told his former coworkers it was from a bullet that grazed him, but the truth was it was from jumping into a pond as a kid and landing on a fallen tree. "You know, after this, you're going to owe me big—like, clearing-my-debt-in-its-entirety big."

Charles, ignoring the remark, said, "I have the town car heading to you. Should be there in less than 20 minutes."

Rex heard a spattering on the window nearest him. The first few drops that were supposed to arrive hours ago pelted the fairway, covering the gold course in shadows. The group of golfers scurried to the golf cart.

"I can drive myself. I'm still sober. Same as last week and the week before that."

"I don't doubt you, but the driver was nearby, so I figured I'd save you the trouble of fighting traffic.

He knew it was a lie, but let it slide. His continual backslides opened him up to comments like that. "Thanks, pal."

"I'm going to have to let you go. The police commissioner has called me twice, and now his secretary is texting me. Rex, please wear a suit. The blue one is the only one you've got that's nearly presentable. I'll call you while you're heading in with details."

"Hey! Wait a minute. What am I walking into here?"

There was a sharp intake of breath on the other end. "Well, you need to solve the whodunit of how a dead body ended up in a room whose only exits were under constant surveillance before the press kills Hitch. The mayor has four senators and a dignitary from a foreign country in for a dinner party for the Chicago elite. They can't have an unsolved murder when Chicago's finest were guarding the place."

"Who bit it?"

"The dignitary's secretary. It happened in the office across the hallway from Mayor Hitch's office— the one his wife uses."

"Yikes." He let out a brief whistle. Grabbing the remote for the TV, he asked, "Are there reporters on the scene?"

"No. Under the mayor's instructions, it's being kept from the press. The M.E. and forensic crew all came in under the radar."

"Yeah, that ain't going to last long with that guest list." He placed the remote back on the coffee table next to a paperback novel, *Death of a Doxy*. "Seriously, none of his group can figure it out, even with all that surveillance?" The protocol for searching everyone coming in and out was put in place during the mayor's first term, after several laptops were alleged to have been stolen by reporters at a party at his mansion. They used them to access internal emails that revealed the inappropriate way the mayor treated his staff. Since then, no one gets in or out without a thorough search.

"I don't have all the details yet, but apparently, they're stumped. If I cared, I'd feel bad for Stevens. That's not the kind of case any detective should have forced on him. I think he was biting his tongue off when he was forced to talk to me to get you down there."

Rex let out a grunt of an unfunny laugh. "The mayor is going to throw a fit when he sees me." He then stood up, reluctantly heading up the stairs to get a quick shower.

"No, he's not." There was a brief silence, and then the sound of the phone came back to his ear. "Whom do you think insisted on getting you down there? He knows your abilities better than anybody."

Without a "goodbye," the phone went silent.

INVESTIGATION HOUR
AND A HALF

Rex—holding an old fedora a former girlfriend gave him and wearing a suit that would appreciate an hour with an iron—jogged through the rain into the town car. Sitting in the back seat was Penny, Charles's legal assistant, giving him an overly optimistic smile.

"Hello, friend!"

As he slid in, he flippantly stated, "So, I need a handler now?"

"Don't be silly. Charles just thought that with all the, ah...previous history that you might like some company."

She smelled like coconuts, and her skin was lightly tanned, except for her fingers. As it always was when he was on a case, his brain already had shifted into hyperdrive, memorizing and noting every detail he encountered. To him, it always felt like flipping on a switch—one that brought him closer to insanity than he wanted to admit. "Well, if I were choosing company, you'd be high on the list." He smiled the smile that his ex-wife used to say could get him anything he wanted. That always made him feel good until she typically added, "...if you didn't always act like such a jerk."

"Ah, you're always so sweet."

Not wanting to engage in her flirting, he asked, "You biking again?"

"Yeah, how did you know?"

"How do you think I know?"

"Oh! Trying to train me again. OK, I'm game. I'd say that you noticed I lost weight."

"You don't look like you lost weight. If you did, I'd have to buy you an anchor, so the wind didn't blow you away." He saw the compliment land even though that wasn't his intention. "Your hands. The tan line stops where your fingers wrap around the handlebars." He folded his own and pointed out the line where the sun would stop shining. "Question is, what are you so nervous about to make you log that much time outdoors, with your busy work schedule?" At best, Rex worked a case a month while he worked on his mental health, but he kept up with Penny weekly. She had impressed him with her intelligence and work ethic the few times they worked together. Penny was one of the few people under 30 whom he knew who gave away nearly all of her free time to her job.

"Just work, life, et cetera. Not everyone lives in an insulated bubble out in the middle of nowhere, like you."

The car took a hard turn as it left the gated community. Rex looked at the shaded dividing glass in the direction of the driver, grimacing. Knowing he couldn't hear, he still called out, "Take it easy, Max!" Being driven and not being able to see directly in front of him always jangled his nerves. "You're mean." He nudged her playfully with his elbow.

She exaggerated his touch playfully, rocking slowly back against the door. "Yeah, that's definitely me. Tell you what—I'll make you a deal: Stop trying to get me to open up, and I won't cross-examine you."

"Do you cross-examine a lot? I thought Charles always settled out of court."

"He definitely has a talent for that."

"Yeah, he really does." Rex settled back into the leather seat, thinking of how many times Charles had talked their way out of difficulties. It was a talent unlike any he'd ever seen. "So, you don't mind babysitting me?"

She gave her first authentic smile, lighting up her face. "That's not why I'm tagging along."

"Look, we both know Charles has you here to keep me in check."

"If that were his intention, he didn't say anything to me. From my point of view, I get to watch you go into the mayor's mansion and show up all his cops. Heh, I'd pay to be there."

Letting it drop, he said, "Well, don't get too excited. They might have this solved before we get there. There are still a few good ones on the force." Rex looked out of the shaded window to his right. He could barely see a few yards out. The rain was increasing as they headed north toward the city. It was still an hour before it got dark, but the streetlights were already on, thanks to the false night the increasing downpour had brought. "Looks like you dragged the rain and gloom with you from the city. It was sunny just a half hour ago."

"Is that why you brought that ridiculous hat along?"

Rex glanced at the old hat sitting on his knee. "No. Brought this to play the part of an authentic gumshoe. You probably don't know what that means, being a youngster and all."

"Yeah, that's sooo you—dressing outlandishly." Smiling and rolling her eyes, Penny grabbed her buzzing phone from her purse. It was Charles. "Yes, sir." Pulling the phone from her ear, she handed it to Rex. "For you."

With his fingertip, he hit the speaker button. "Hey."

"Why didn't you answer your phone?"

Rex patted himself down. "Crap. I left it on my dresser." It was a familiar habit. The instrument had become a symbol of the outside world from which he had been hiding. "Good thing Penny's here. She can handle my communications."

"One of these days, you and I are going to have a serious talk." There was a deep sigh. "All right, here's what I got so far."

Rex leaned back and took in all the information, storing it in the forefront of his mind. Each time he did this, the weight of a great burden seemed to seep into his bones, weighing him down. With the information, new memories and feelings would form, and they'd surface every time he recalled the scene. What started as a mnemonic device had grown into an increasingly unstable emotional state. Reminding himself that Charles was worth the pain, he processed the information, realizing that unless there were significant gaps in what was being reported, there was a high likelihood that he couldn't add anything to the detectives' conclusions.

INVESTIGATION HOUR TWO
AND FIFTEEN MINUTES

The town car pulled up to 442 Madison Street. There was an open space cleared for visitors directly in front of the enormous century-and-a-quarter-old brick structure, which looked out of place among the glass skyscrapers to its right. The building was a reminder of what the city used to be and how far it had come. In the shadow of the building, the street was lined with uniformed cops. Frustration was etched into every line of their faces that poked out from their rain gear. Rex could remember the days when he was stuck in all kinds of weather at the mayor's whim. He never resented them, but sure didn't miss them now.

Penny reached for the door, then Rex quickly leaned over and grabbed her hand. She tilted her head, raising her eyebrows inquisitively.

"Don't. They'll come to the car. It's their procedure. With everything going on, we don't need the troops rushing us."

On cue, a female officer with a bulletproof vest held an umbrella beside a tall, thin man who looked as if he hadn't eaten in days. Penny rolled down the window.

Rex thought he had curbed all his feelings,

yet his nerves were tightening the closer he got to getting into some real work. Having to walk the high wire again was prompting him to want to get into a pissing match with the lieutenant at the car door. However, he knew that playing the resentment game and taking shots at his former colleagues would only slow him down, and he wanted to get this over with and return to his cocoon far away from here as soon as possible, so he clenched his teeth.

He wanted a drink so badly that it felt like he could taste the phantom fumes from the last one he had over a month ago on the roof of his mouth. "Hey, Stevens."

"Rex, thanks for coming out." His polite tone didn't match his glare. The lieutenant grabbed the handle of the door, stepping aside to allow Penny space under the umbrella. The second the rain hit him, the comb-over on top of his head quickly showed gaps of pasty skin as the thin strands were pushed aside.

Following Penny out of the car, Rex yanked the hat down over his eyebrows to shield himself from the cameras and hunched-over reporters held back by a line of officers. Recognition was apparent in Penny's stare at why he brought his disguise. As soon as he got out, his coat was soaking wet in less than a few seconds. Beyond the late spring dampness, he could smell onions from the hot dog vendor at the corner. The ancient man with a wild mane of white hair was cowering under his umbrella. He was a fixture in the neighborhood, going back to Rex's teenage years, bringing back memories of ballgames and school. So much had changed in the city that the memories felt like they belonged to someone else.

Rex's eyes swept the building, keeping his face obscured under the hat's brim and noting the surveillance cameras in the gables. Nothing seemed to have changed since his previous visit. A few of the assembled officers grunted and nodded as he made his way up the stone stairs to the building's oversized doors. They were so high that a semi could pull in without slowing down. Walking through metal detectors, he remembered the article he had read when the mayor had them installed after a young man snuck in with a knife, thinking it would help his protest get a hearing. Wondering how the staff felt about not only having their bags searched every day as they reported to work, but also going through the detectors, he was happy he had left his own gun back at the townhouse. He held a concealed-carry license, but knew that his former colleagues still would've hassled him—some for good reason, others because that was their way.

In the foyer, the kinetic mess that was a crime scene put Rex's senses on overload. He made a quick mental impression of all that he saw before focusing on the various conversations. A therapist he once visited, in the hopes of relieving his chronic hyperactivity, told him that the human brain was only capable of listening to one single conversation at a time. He asked how he could then repeat verbatim multiple ones that took place simultaneously. She said he seemed to have a unique ability to cycle back in and out of them quickly. Using this ability, he heard smart-ass comments by his former coworkers, as well as some useless chatter.

He tried to pretend that he couldn't hear the comments of the people whom he, at one time, would have given his life for, but it was growing more difficult. Rearranging his face, he shook the rain off his shoulders—small puddles formed on the veined marble floor.

Stevens carefully ran a comb through his thin hair before saying, "We have a desk in a spare room on the fourth floor for you to start in."

This close, he smelled of aftershave and cigar smoke. "I want to examine the office where the stabbing took place first."

"Forensics has been through it already. We have the reports ready for you…at your desk."

Rex took in air through his nose and slowly let it out. Taking a step closer, he spoke in a near-whisper. "Look, you don't want me here, and I don't want to be here. It's awkward. I get it. But understand that I don't want to go up there to double-check what your team has done. However, I need to go into that room. It's just the way I work. So, please, let's just go up there and skip the part where we both measure our dicks before we end up in the same place: with me going where I want anyway.

OK?" Rex slouched slightly so their eyes would be level.

"Now, I'm going to step back and let you order me to go up there. You're in charge here. I respect that. I'm just here to consult. I honestly feel for you. If this were my investigation, the last thing I'd want is for some washed-up detective coming in and reviewing everything I did." Rex stepped back and continued to remove water from his suit.

Stevens rolled his tongue inside his closed mouth, making a large bulge in his stubble-filled cheek. "Thinking it over, yeah, I think it would be best for you to see the office first. Might be beneficial for you to get up to speed by talking to *my* team instead of just reading *my* reports."

"Sounds good."

Stevens turned and walked toward a narrow hallway. Rex nodded at Penny to follow. Passing artwork that cost more than a year of his highest salary, he whispered to her, "Having fun?"

Looking up at the lieutenant, she said, "I don't like him."

"More than a few have said that, but I'll give him this much: He's in a tough spot."

"It's not just that. I don't trust any man who dyes his hair. It's a sign he isn't in tune with his own mortality."

Rex gave her an appreciative smile as they caught up to the lieutenant standing in front of an oddly sized door in the shape of a very narrow rectangle.

In what looked like a coat closet was a cramped elevator with a web of metal-crossed doors. Stevens pressed the tiny button that was nearly hidden in the patterned wallpaper.

Rex straightened his tie, noticing a soup stain that must've been made a year ago. He rubbed it with his damp finger, which did nothing but accentuate the discoloration. "Since this morning, who has been in the room where the murder occurred?" This elicited an offended look on the lieutenant's face, as if he'd asked when was the last time Stevens slept with his wife, and not a relevant question—a look that said: *Who are you to ask me anything?* As the elevator groaned from somewhere above, it was easy to see the struggle on his face— the struggle of duty vs. ego that hindered so many in authority.

His tongue worked over his cheek again. With his lips barely parting, he spat out, "Staff mainly."

"Specifically, who and what were they doing in the room?"

Stevens, never looking at Rex, pulled out his phone and scrolled down. Sounding like a disinterested waiter giving orders to a short-order cook, he quickly said, "Maid this morning at 9 a.m. Assuming she was cleaning. That can be confirmed in the report that you don't want to read." Squinting, a web of fine wrinkles surrounded his eyes. "Calvin Litimer, the butler, came in an hour later with a service cart, as was his routine, bringing in pastries and tea. Hitch's wife uses the room as an office, as I believe you know, and whether she shows up or not, he brings the food in." He gave a quick eye roll. "After that, Ms. Jackson began her shift at 10 a.m., and then Mr. Gavin, the victim, reported to work at precisely 10:42 a.m."

"Did either of them bring anything into the room?"

"Notes don't state it."

"Can you find out?"

"I can find out anything I want. I'm in cha —" He then shook his head like a parent catching themselves before berating a child, staring daggers at Rex as his tongue worked over the inside of his cheek again.

After a loud whining sound and slight vibration, the door opened. They crammed inside the space that appeared to be built for two very slender people. Rex pressed against the wall. "Who's running the scene?"

"Bradley."

"Good choice." He meant it. She was, by far, the most capable detective he had worked with while he was on the force. "How long have you been at it?"

He glanced at his smartwatch. "Four hours now."

Rex bit back, asking why he was called in, already knowing how impatient the mayor was. Even without any substantial physical evidence, the detectives should be given some time to work. Instead, he took a stab. "Hitch must be blowing his lid."

The elevator creaked along so slowly that Rex wondered why they didn't just walk up. Suddenly, he remembered the wall of windows at the main staircase, and it came to him: Stevens didn't want the press to get a picture of him next to Rex.

"You know his ambitions. He can't have Washington or the press thinking poorly of him." Pressing the elevator button several times in a row, as if it would hasten its ascent, he added, "Look, I really appreciate you coming out, but I'm telling you, you're not going to make any more progress than we have. Don't take that the wrong way. I know how good you are, really, but there's nothing left to find."

"I only got a short description of what happened here, but from what I heard, I agree with you."

"Really?" The detective's face went slack, smoothing out his wrinkled forehead and making him look a decade younger.

"Yeah. You're up against it on this one."

The elevator came to a sudden stop, jostling them up and down. For a quarter of a second, Rex thought they were going back down, and then the door finally opened. Half a dozen uniformed officers stood around holding foam cups. In unison, they all looked at him. He gave a quick nod and immediately scanned the room. There was one large window with a closed, heavy drape directly behind the collection of cops. Flanking them were two closed doors. From previous visits, Rex knew the one on the left was the mayor's office. The other room on the right was the room Mayor Hitch's wife used as an office. Its door was wide open, and most of the voices he heard came from that direction. The rug covering the wood floor in the hallway was thick and looked like it had come from Asia decades ago. Thinking of his wet shoes, he cringed, wondering how old and expensive the rug was.

"Before you go in, I need you to sign this." Stevens pulled a folded document from his inner breast pocket.

Rex reached out to grab it, but Penny quickly intercepted it, saying, "What's this?"

"Nondisclosure agreement. It's standard boilerplate for any, ah, consultant."

"Uh-huh." Penny, while reading, muttered. "Yeah, we'll see about that."

Rex asked the man he used to report to, "Well, while she's reviewing that, you comfortable telling me one thing that's not going to be on any report?"

"Depends."

"Fair enough. You know the security detail who were standing guard personally?"

"No."

"New to the post?"

"'Bout a week on this detail, but has been on the force for nearly 10 years. He's a lifer just like his old man." He patted his hair down ever so carefully. "We questioned him. He's clean—frankly, maybe too clean. Perfect record until now. I mean, not that we can blame him for anything here. Even if we thought he was involved somehow, the cameras would've shown him going into the room."

Rex studied the statue in the corner and the tiny glass eye just above it that he knew had a camera lens built in.

Penny said, "You don't have to sign it. My guess is, they won't do anything if you don't, but if you want to, it's OK to sign."

Rex, without glancing at it, grabbed the pen and scribbled his name, knowing this was all for show because a nondisclosure was necessary; Penny would have to sign one as well. Heading to the room where the death had taken place, a very familiar sense overtook him.

INVESTIGATION HOUR TWO
AND FORTY MINUTES

Bradley, with a sincere smile, put down a tablet and walked up to Rex, wearing worn jeans and a blazer that had her badge on the lapel. Pushing her wavy hair from her face, a few strands got stuck in her faded lipstick as she said, "It's good to see you."

She reached out her hand, which had a small tattoo of a butterfly popping out from her sleeve. As Rex shook it, he noticed her missing wedding ring. He remembered hearing a rumor that her wife had custody of their child and had moved away. Knowing this wasn't the time or place for that kind of talk, he responded, "You as well."

She leaned against a very cluttered desk, shaking her hand as if it were cold. Responsibility was etched in her face, but it didn't diminish the intelligence in her eyes. "So, how much do you know?"

Appreciating her habit of getting right down to business, he responded. "If it's all right with you, let's pretend as if nothing."

"Figured you'd say that." She pulled her hair to the right side, resting it on her shoulder. "You want coffee or anything?"

He shook his head. Looking at Penny, he raised

his eyebrows.

"No, thanks."

"Bradley, this is Penny, my—"

"Lawyer." Penny shot her hand forward briskly, shaking the detective's hand.

Bradley wiped her palm on her jeans. Rex noticed, remembering she had bouts of germaphobia that usually only surfaced when she worked. Quirks like that came with a job that constantly forced you to face death. Rex used to work with a desk sergeant who thought he was a philosopher. He had a theory that if hanging around with the reaper didn't alter your normal behavior, that was a bigger problem than drinking or acting a little peculiar because it meant you had a few screws loose to begin with.

Bradley recoiled her hand, saying a little too loudly, "All right, intros out of the way, and nobody wants refreshments. What we got here is the deceased found by Ms. Jackson in a room that had seemingly no entry."

As she was winding up to continue, Stevens spoke over her. "Thanks. I need you down on the second floor to be there for the interview with Ms. Jackson."

"Peter, that's a follow-up interview. I already spoke to her." She stood up straight, taking a slight step forward.

"Yeah, I know. I want you there."

Her head jerked back as if she had been struck by a strong wind. "What about briefing Rex?"

"Detective Cliffe can handle that."

He wasn't surprised by the lieutenant's unprofessional manner. Stevens was a good cop in the sense that he didn't cut any corners in an investigation, but he couldn't slow down his pettiness, which made him a bad leader.

"Really?" She stared him down for nearly half a minute. "Whatever you say, boss." She then stomped out of the room.

As soon as she crossed the threshold, Detective Cliffe entered. He pulled at his belt, which had slipped beneath his paunch, tugging hard. With a toothpick stuck in the corner of his mouth just beneath a mustache that looked like a thick, folded sock, he smiled and laughed. "Well, if it ain't Chicago's missin' star."

Listening to the accent that was so thick, it made Chicago sound like three separate words, Rex clenched his teeth. He glanced at Stevens, noting his self-satisfied smirk, making him want to knock their heads together.

"So, I guess, ah, you're here to show us how dumb we are, like the old days, huh?"

"Good to see you too, Ronald." The clown jokes had followed the detective since early in his career.

"Don't call me that!"

"OK...*Detective*. If you could be so kind, perhaps you could give me a status report?"

"Yeah, sure. Who's the broa—ah, lady with ya?"

"This is Penny. She works for Charles."

Cliffe looked at Stevens, hooking a thumb at the young lawyer. "You good with this, boss?"

"Yeah. Give him everything."

"Okie dokie." He gripped the toothpick and dug steadily, like he was retracting a full pork chop. When his mouth was settled, he flipped open a tablet and read aloud. "Mr. Gavin was stabbed. The instrument had a circumference of approximately half an inch." His thick fingers mimed the size.

He pointed to the corpse on the floor. "That's obviously him. The murder weapon was, ah, inserted into his chest near the heart. Toxicology did a super rush job. Shows no poison, meaning death most likely came from the impalement. Ms. Jackson entered exactly two minutes after 4. Windows were locked from the inside. They got sensors, cheap run-of-the-mill Sylvester brand, but no apparent tampering. The front door to the office was closed and locked at 2 by Gavin after Ms. Jackson left for an errand. Doors have sensors, just like the windows, and there's a camera in the vestibule. It didn't open until Ms. Jackson came back from her errand and discovered the deceased."

He paused, taking a quick breath as though the reading was winding him. "No usable prints anywhere. Initially, we all figured whoever did him went out the window and found a workaround to the sensor, ya know. Outdoor camera shows nothing but pelting rain, and the floor was bone dry for confirmation. Beyond that, if you're thinking whoever did it tricked the camera, the sensor, and

Mother Nature and scaled up to the roof, we had four good cops up there as surveillance, with the guest list being what it is. If the killer scaled down, he would've been on top of the glass ceiling of the greenhouse. The mayor's wife had guests in that room, so they surely would've seen and heard someone."

Rex playfully said, "That's it? And you don't have a collar yet?"

Cliffe let out a good, hard, patronizing laugh that got the attention of the officers in the vestibule. "That's why you're here…wonder boy."

Rex scanned the corpse and the area surrounding him. "Good one." The body was lying on its side, with its arms drawn near the chest, as if it were clutching a wound. The streaks of blood, streaming in several directions, shot across the carpet. Carefully avoiding the evidence, he stood near the position where Gavin would've been when he was attacked. Mimicking a knife, he pulled it toward himself and then outward, flaying open his fingers. "Did the blood spatter folks say the attack came from behind?"

"You're the super sleuth. Whattaya think?"

"Looks like a clean flow to me. No interruption as it sprayed." Rex pivoted his left foot. "Angle would've been about here." He swept with his hand near his waist. "Plunged from behind, and then the instrument was removed quickly, hence the clear stream."

"Yeah, that's what Roberts said."

Rex had worked with the head medical examiner in the past and knew him to be top-notch. Glad that he'd be getting accurate intel, he said, "With a cut that deep, and your man just outside the door, he says he didn't hear anything?"

"Apparently not."

"Interesting."

"The attacker could've cupped his mouth first to stifle any noise."

Rex, picturing the attack, asked, "Why do I smell bleach?"

"There were trace amounts found on the victim's hands from a sanitizing cloth we found on the floor. It was doused in blood."

Rex extended his hand, reaching for Cliffe's tablet. "Do you mind?"

"Suit yourself."

Rex went through the report, skipping over what he already knew. The only anomaly he came across was that the deceased's blood had shown he was terminally ill.

"Gavin was pretty sick?"

"Yeah, but Robert is confident that ain't what killed him."

You think so, genius? Rex cycled through one more time. "Where are the crime scene photos?"

"Ain't uploaded to the server yet. If you really need one, Bradley has the originals on her tablet."

Rex asked, "What's your team's theory regarding the bleach?"

"Ain't got a good one. Maybe he was a clean

freak, maybe OCD, something like that, and over-washed his hands, but he ain't used the toilet since entering. So, the theory has some holes, but can still fit."

Rex handed the tablet back. "So, Gavin was the private secretary for… " The president's name from Charles's debriefing popped into his mind as it always did. "Mr. Samath?"

"In a way, correct."

"What does that mean?" Rex was looking over the area around Gavin's body. There wasn't a single smear of blood behind him, only in front of him. The blood had obviously been stepped in. Rex looked at the bottom of Gavin's shoes. There was smeared blood.

"He was officially a bodyguard, but Samath calls all his people secretaries."

Rex bent down to get closer to the corpse. Near the wound, the smearing of blood made him question whether the instrument that killed him had been wiped clean after the wound was made. "In a place this big, why did they put him in the room with the mayor's wife's secretary? There has to be another spare desk somewhere in this place." He glanced at Stevens.

"He was here as a guard."

"Guarding what?"

Stevens, pulling his coat from his suit jacket, said, "Excuse me," then walked away.

Rex nodded to Cliffe. "Guarding what?"

"Let the boss answer that."

"Fair enough. What did Mr. Samath's security say about this man's background?"

Cliffe nervously looked at Stevens, who was laying into whoever was on the other end of the phone. The detective finally said, "Nothing."

"They're not cooperating with the investigation?"

"Yeah, uh, we haven't told them yet."

"What?"

Stevens held up his hands in a halting motion. Barking orders, he hung up. "Look, man. Mayor's call, not ours. There are some extenuating circumstances."

"There better be."

"As I said, it's not my place to tell the mayor how to run his household and office."

"It is when there's a murder here, buddy. What's the plan here? To solve the crime, then tell him? For what, to save face? Deflecting blame or incompetence?" Stevens was rubbing the back of his neck, a telltale sign he was about to blow. Rex slowed down. "OK, so, what do we know about him?"

"The background check we did when we were made aware of their visit shows that he's worked for Samath for a little more than two decades. Seems like an upstanding citizen. He has no wife or children. Seems to be a Boy Scout. He's dedicated his life to upholding the politics of his country. He enlisted and, after 15 years of well-decorated service, became part of the security team. I can give you the full report if you want to read it, but I assure you that you aren't going to find anything useful."

Rex stood looking at the wall to the left of the desk. "You guys got any hunches?"

Cliffe responded. "Just the obvious ones. Only real choice is Jackson. She was the only one in here, if only for a brief second."

"Help me understand that. Isn't she ruled out by time of death and the fact that both the camera and Winnipeg's account confirm she was in the room for less than 20 seconds before she screamed?"

"Yeah, but maybe she had a clever way of pulling it off. Before she got here, the camera was on the entire time, proving no one else entered. Winnipeg was in view the entire time, so he was clear unless he shot a dissolving dart through a closed door that left no hole, and it hit dead center."

Rex stifled a few quips, saying, "Is that a hatch?" He waved to a small door about waist level next to the main door. "A dumbwaiter?"

"Yeah. This used to be the main bedroom before it was converted into an office. Save your breath. It didn't move from the second floor. First off, the motor's been burnt out for months. Apparently, maintenance has been having trouble finding a replacement. Second, there's a camera on the floor below showing it sitting idle all afternoon."

"Was the dumbwaiter used much before it stopped working?"

"I, uh, didn't ask. Why would I?"

Rex considered replying, *Maybe it was purposely disabled to make it necessary to have extra people enter the room today,* but thought better of it. Instead, he headed to the door and lifted it with the sleeve of his shirt. Looking up into the dark shaft, he saw what he believed to be the rafters to the roof of the mansion with a wheel and motor attached to them. Examining the tight space, there was no conceivable way anyone could exit through there. Looking down, he saw the top of a wooden box with a thick cable attached. Convinced no one could escape through the shaft, he asked, "No camera active in this room? Is that typical?"

"It's an office. The mayor's orders are not to have cameras in any rooms or offices. Only hallways. You can guess why."

Rex dusted off his sleeve as he walked back to the center of the room. "With all those artifacts in here, you'd think they'd be slightly more diligent with security. What's all that stuff, anyway?" He pointed to the tiered mahogany shelving.

"Mayor's wife has a tradition of exchanging... uh, gifts with visitors. They bring her this junk, and she exchanges items from her private collections."

Rex, looking over the eclectic antiques, walked to a polished silver tray holding a coffee decanter and foam cups. It was nestled between a kaleidoscope on a stand and a statue of the head of a very unattractive man. "What's usually here?"

"What's that?"

"Cliffe, on this shelf that the coffee tray is sitting on." Rex pointed to the carafe and cups. "What was on the shelf before the tray replaced it?"

"How would I know that?"

"Well, there's a missing murder weapon, and whatever was sitting on this display isn't here." He mimed, looking around the area. "I might think you'd make it your business to know that, or possibly now ask who removed it from the scene."

"Butler brought the coffee in. Watched him myself."

"OK, when he put the tray down, what was here, and where did he put it?"

"Instead of interrogating me, how about you look over the notes from Ms. Jackson's interview?" His shoulders went up like a boxer's trying to intimidate his opponent as a deep vein bulged in his neck. "That would be a ton more productive than messing with me."

Rex's lips parted. He then remembered the promise he made to himself to try to get out of there as fast as possible. Turning, he said, "Stevens, did the lab guys get a picture of the room? We need to know what was here. Perhaps one of your hardworking group in the hallway could get on it." He nodded at the officers who were chatting about the crosstown rivalry game, currently postponed at Wrigley Field between the Cubs and White Sox.

"I'll handle my own." Stevens's tongue then worked over his cheek again, squinting. "So, you're up to speed now. Unless you've got something of interest to add to move things along, how about I show you to your office?"

Ignoring the lieutenant, he asked, "Have you

interviewed the butler?"

"Why?"

"Well, he was in the room before the murder and after. Besides Ms. Jackson, who else from the staff was?"

Stevens looked at Cliffe. "Do you know?"

"Before we got here? Other than the mayor, I can't say for sure without reviewing the notes."

Stevens asked Rex, "Where you going with this?"

He wanted to say "*doing your job*," but instead whispered, "Maybe nowhere." Rex scanned the shelves. The second row comprised dolls in various colors and styles. He knew nothing of this type of collecting, but each porcelain replica looked expensive, covered in ornamental jewelry. The tier above it was full of assorted collectors' items, mostly statuettes, eclectic trinkets, and an enormous globe sitting on the floor all the way to the right. Looking up to the left, he saw a painting of a ship at sea. "Cliffe, did you look inside the safe?"

He eyed his boss.

Stevens answered for his subordinate. "How do you know there's a safe?"

"Because in a house filled with original artwork, that painting is an obvious fake, and it's crooked with slight dirt marks on the plaster where someone's hand keeps touching. If you don't have the combo, I suggest you get it and see what, if anything, is missing. Or, at the very least, dust it for prints."

"It's already been dusted, and the mayor himself checked the contents. Why would you assume something is missing?" Stevens didn't hide the rising anger in his voice. "This room had been under surveillance, and the only person who could have smuggled something out is lying there behind you."

"Because the robber who killed this man most likely cleaned it out unless he orchestrated all of this for one of the collectibles on those shelves."

Cliffe loudly said, "Oh, so now it's a robbery! Why didn't we think of that? Oh, I know, because nothing was stolen!"

Rex walked over to Penny. Cliffe was hitching his pants again, his outburst apparently loosening something. The detective's gaze settled on Penny's chest. Rex, no longer caring about etiquette, whispered, "I bet I can get him kicked outta here in under a minute."

Her bottom lip parted, noticing Cliffe's glare. "Sounds like a great idea to me."

Rex's tone shifted, antagonizing the man. "Don't know why you didn't think of it. It's pretty obvious to anyone paying attention. Stevens, when's Bradley coming back? I need someone who can keep up."

Cliffe grabbed his belt, tugging the waistline up an inch into his large midsection. "Listen here, *pal*. Your buddy Charles ain't here to protect you, like in the old days. Keep it up, and we'll see where it gets ya."

"Probably promoted past you, Ronald."

Stevens raised his hands. "All right, that's enough!" His bellow was loud enough that the collection of officers in the hallway all went silent.

"I agree, boss, it's time to get this waste of space out of here." Cliffe strode across the room and reached for Rex's lapel. Rex swiftly grabbed Cliffe's wrist and, with a quick twist, nearly had the rotund man tumbling to the floor. He grabbed him by the belt at the last second, keeping Cliffe upright. Tugging, he said, "Careful there. You might hurt yourself."

Stevens screamed, "Knock it off!"

"Tell that to the help. Your boy here is going to get himself into trouble one of these days with that temper of his." Rex patted the man's bulging stomach and whispered, "No wonder your old lady runs around on you."

With his eyebrow twitching, Cliffe took a swing. Rex stepped into it, and the blow, having no force without a proper wind-up, glanced off the side of his neck. Pushing back, he shouted, "Lieutenant, you going to handle this, or should I?"

"Cliffe! Out now!"

"Stevens, you saw it!"

"Out!"

"Son of a bitch!" He elbowed Rex as he left the room. When he reached the hall, the plainclothes officers parted, letting him pass.

Rex looked at Penny with an expression that said, *You see what I used to have to deal with?* Penny, being polite as she always was, never changed her expression. Rex almost felt pity for the detective who got his job through nepotism. He never held it against Cliffe that he leapfrogged past other, more-qualified candidates. In the machine that was politics in a city this large, it wasn't unusual. What bothered Rex was that Cliffe didn't take advantage of the tremendous opportunity and learn the job.

Stevens angrily said, "Time for you to get to your office, Haining."

"I'm not done yet."

"Oh, yes, you are, Rex."

Shaking his head, Rex said, "No, and you know it." As he walked toward the collection on the shelves, he slowly looked over each item, looking for any trace that anything had been moved.

Stevens erupted. "Look—" He bit off his sentence when the mayor entered the room.

Dressed in a tuxedo, Hitch had an officer trailing behind who weighed nearly 250 pounds, busting out of a bargain-aisle suit and keeping stride with him. Watching them from the corner of his eye, Rex thought the man should be exempt from the skinny-jeans trend for the sake of everyone who had to look at him.

Mayor Hitch asked in a very practiced tone, "What's with all the commotion?"

Stevens quickly responded. "Nothing, sir. Just working out some details of the case."

Hitch walked up to Rex and offered his hand.

Reluctantly, Rex shook it. He thought he'd

have more anger, but instead, there was mainly tiredness—the tiredness that usually only came after working a 20-hour shift.

"I appreciate you coming. I really do."

The look of false sincerity brought a dozen snide remarks to mind. Wanting to get down to business, he asked, "Sir, can you please open the safe?"

"Yes, but why? I already checked it earlier. Nothing was missing."

Rex stepped to the side. "Just being thorough." He grabbed a pair of rubber gloves off the desktop that were in an overflowing cardboard box. "If you don't mind, please wear these."

The mayor gave him a sly, superior look he had mastered in his many years of defeating political opponents. He pulled a single glove onto his well-manicured right hand before pulling the painting open. It moved to the right on hinges, revealing a safe built into the wood-paneled wall. "If you don't mind, I'd prefer not to reprogram the safe."

Getting the hint, Rex grunted and looked in the opposite direction, then stepped closer to Penny.

Leaning in, she said, "Hopefully, you find the knife soon—to cut the tension."

He wanted to laugh, but could only muster a pathetic shrug.

"Seriously, do you have this figured out already?"

His eyebrows rose into high arches as he shook his head. "Not...really, but I have a theory."

"Play nice, then. OK?"

He appreciated her looking out for him, even if it felt awkward, but right now, her concern seemed out of place. She wished she knew him better for his previous work so she could have confidence that he'd do whatever was necessary to get the job done, rather than the person he had become, as he let her comment die. "Do me a favor. Find out as much as you can about Helen Jackson—background, who she dates, anything you can get off the Internet."

She pulled out her phone. "On it."

Rex nodded his thanks. He asked over his shoulder in the direction of the mayor. "Sir, what do you keep in there?"

"Some personal effects." There was the sound of the dial spinning. "Legal papers and some cash." A familiar click of the door opening filled the room. "Tonight, we have a necklace from one of our Sri Lankan guests for safekeeping."

Stevens folded his arms. In all the years Rex worked for the man, he could count on one hand the number of times he saw him smile. He typically didn't judge him, knowing the pressure the job put on anyone, except when Stevens would lash out at the dedicated people who worked for him. Rex's patience then grew thinner.

From behind, they heard the mayor exclaim. "Well, Mr. Haining, just what were you expecting to find? Everything appears to be here, like before."

Turning around, Rex saw what he had been

expecting. Walking toward the safe, he said, "Mind if I take a closer look inside?"

The mayor stepped to the side. "Be my guest."

Rex lifted a gold necklace with a sizable ruby at its center, using his sleeve as a glove. He held it up to the light, twirling it. Kneeling, he brought it to the floor's surface.

The mayor asked, "What're you doing?"

Rex scratched it across the tile floor. A red line was embedded where the ruby had scraped. "Stevens, can you have someone send in an evidence bag?"

The mayor grabbed at the necklace with his ungloved hand. "Haining, wait a minute."

Rex turned around, shielding the jewel from him. "Please, sir, don't touch this."

"You don't understand. That belongs to one of my guests. Its value to him and his people cannot be easily explained."

"I perfectly understand, and that's why I'm going to now ask Mr. Stevens to not allow anyone in or out of the house while we try to determine how this was switched out with a fake." Rex held it up and studied it in the light.

The mayor's eyes lit up. "What?"

"See that red line across the porcelain tile?" Rex pointed to the floor. "If this were a real ruby, it would've scratched the floor, not left that mark."

A uniformed officer came in with a clear evidence bag. She held it open as Rex placed the necklace inside. "Now, Mr. Stevens, would you kindly tell me what was removed when the butler brought the coffee tray in?"

Stevens looked at the officer and barked, "Get Bradley up here!"

Sealing the bag, she said, "Yes, sir."

Mayor Hitch was rubbing the bottom of his jaw so intensely that it looked like he was applying an unseen lotion. "So, the man who killed Gavin also got into my safe?" His face bunched. "But no one knows the combination other than me."

Rex quickly said, "Let's not assume it was a man. What about your wife?"

Penny cringed. Rex added, "Strike that! No offense there, honestly. I'm not implying she had anything to do with this."

The mayor stopped his jaw work and meticulously straightened his suit jacket. "*No.* She doesn't know it. There's nothing of substantial value in there, so I never thought to tell her."

"Why was there a ruby in there?"

"Mr. Samath asked me to store it."

"That's why Gavin was here—to guard this?" Fuming, Rex looked at Stevens, wondering how he could be so narrow-minded that he'd keep such a vital detail hidden. "Well?"

The mayor nodded. His face went slack as if the gravity of the situation had finally settled in on him.

"Where's Samath now?"

Lowering his voice, the mayor said, "He had an appointment on the north side."

Rex could see he was hiding something. The mayor's left eye twitched, the same way it did when he made an impossible campaign promise. "Did he leave any other security behind?"

"Not that I'm aware of. Stevens?" He raised his eyebrows, emphasizing the question.

Stevens looked at his tablet. Squinting, he finally pulled out a cheap pair of glasses. "Don't believe so. One second. No. They all went with him to his meeting." He quickly returned the glasses to his pocket.

Rex ran through the briefing earlier from Charles. The words were there, floating in his mind, as if they were printed on paper. Everything was close, but he couldn't quite see the complete answer yet. What he did see didn't seem possible, yet he knew it had to be the answer. He walked across the room and stopped near Penny. Inspecting the desktop, he turned and asked Stevens, "Is the dumbwaiter used often?"

The mayor said, "It was until it stopped working. The staff would send up my wife's food so it would stay warm, as the kitchen is two floors below in the basement."

"When exactly was it reported not to be working, Stevens?"

"I'm not sure. If it's relevant, I'll find out."

Rex brought his hand to his chin. His eyes moved from the coffee tray to the safe. "Please do." He tilted his head to the side, measuring the distance. "Mr. Hitch, you're sure no one else has the combination to this safe?"

"My wife and I did before I changed it last."

It wasn't surprising to Rex that Hitch would change the password even with nothing of value in there. His remarkable paranoia was whispered about behind his back by all who knew him well —just like the rumors of his corruption. "You sure nobody else? Sorry, not doubting you. I mean, is it jotted down on a piece of paper that someone could access?"

"No, I can safely say I have it only in my memory. I'm quite sure I never told anyone else, including my wife. I remember because when I changed it last year, I meant to tell her and never got around to it."

Stevens interrupted, "Haining, did you ever consider it was picked?"

Rex barked back, "That safe is top of the line. If it was picked, then where's the equipment?"

Rex could feel Stevens' shame from across the room. Even though it was a taste of his own medicine, it brought him no joy. "Mayor, this one's a little harder to answer, so please do your best to remember every exact detail. When you opened it to place the ruby inside, was anyone positioned where they could see you open it?"

The mayor squinted as he looked at the dead man lying on the ground. "Wait, are you saying—"

"I'm just trying to get an idea of what happened here."

"No, the ah...deceased was in the room, but

there's no way he could've seen me enter the combo."

"Who else was there?"

"Mr. Samath. He handed me the necklace, and he had two additional security guards."

"Why did Samath ask you to lock it away?"

"Beyond the ruby's value, it has a kind of spiritual meaning for Mr. Samath and his people. As he explained it to me, the man who wears it is granted wisdom beyond his years, giving them the ability to lead their nation. It's a custom of theirs to pass the ruby to each new regime."

"Then why did he remove it?"

The mayor glanced at his watch. "In his country, it's now night. As is the custom, he can only wear it during daylight hours. At night, he takes it off. That's where Mr. Gavin came in. His only job was to guard the necklace. He apparently did it every night. That's how strong their belief is in the man who wears it."

Rex glanced at Mr. Gavin. "Tough result for an easy detail." He shook his head. The hypothesis was solidifying. "When you placed the ruby in the safe, could the other two security guards see you enter the combination?"

"No. They never fully entered the room. They were in the lobby with Samath in front of the elevator." Hitch walked to the safe, then pointed to the open door. You see, from here, there isn't the slightest possibility they could have seen me enter the combination. Believe me—I checked."

Rex had no doubt, witnessing firsthand over

the years the mayor's desire for extreme privacy. "Earlier, when I asked if anyone else had been in the room, how come you failed to mention it, Stevens?"

"We kept it out of the report."

"Why?!"

"Because Samath and his handlers, when we were discussing security, asked for discretion regarding the handling of the jewel. Apparently, it's a point of contention in his country. Some view the ritual as necessary, and others frown on it."

Knowing better than to get into a conversation about politics—even when it involved efficient police work—Rex said, "Stevens, I need to see Calvin Litimer."

The mayor interjected. "Why do you need to see my butler? I can assure you he's an upstanding citizen. He'd never be part of this...this dirty business."

"I'm not saying he was, but he has access to this house, the safe, and most likely removed the murder weapon."

The mayor's security guard handed him a phone. "Sir, you might want to take this."

Hitch held the phone near his waist. "What's Litimer's involvement in this?"

"I'm not prepared to discuss that until I have the opportunity to interview him."

Glancing at the face of the phone, he dismissively whispered, "Very well. Stevens, please accommodate the interview." He disappeared into the sea of police in the lobby, saying, "Sorry to keep you waiting, senator. I'll be right down."

After the lieutenant barked his orders to get Litimer into a nearby office, Rex asked, "Stevens, are all visitors and staff still logged and searched, or do a few get waived around?"

His smarminess was now absent from his face. Being bested by Rex left him looking wounded. "Yeah."

"Even with all this commotion?"

"Their logs indicate they do." He stopped; it was evident that a thought came to him quickly. "As far as smuggling something out, the logs show no one leaving. We reviewed the video footage, as well as interviewed the security guards, per Bradley's request."

"What about side entrances?"

"All locked and under video surveillance, except for the parlor's side door that leads into the garden. That one is open. It has a camera on it, though. The courtyard is enclosed by 10-foot-high, ivy-covered brick walls. There are no cameras out there." He cycled through his tablet. "As far as what the video shows, Ms. Jackson, Mr. Litimer, and two others have gone outside since the body was discovered—all to smoke on the terrace. None at the same time." He closed the lid of the tablet and traced his hand slowly over it before looking up. "Rex, it's got to be Jackson, right?"

His openness felt like old times, when some mutual respect was still present. Rex gave a shrug.

Bradley walked into the room and glanced at

the safe, then at Stevens. "The plot thickens, huh?"

Rex said, "Apparently. What was on the display rack before the coffee was placed there?"

She typed her password into her laptop, holding it up at eye level with her left hand. A couple of seconds later, she turned the computer around.

The last place on the display was occupied by a very human-looking doll. Rex, for a minute, remembered a story he once read of a burglary that was committed by a tiny woman who snuck in disguised as a doll. He shook the thought out of his head, knowing it wasn't a consideration. "Can you pull up the footage of Jackson leaving the room?"

"On it." She spun the computer around and typed furiously on the keys.

Rex turned, then glanced out the window. Sheets of rain were beating against the glass. The rhythmic patter was growing loud enough so that he could barely hear the cops in the lobby. He looked at Stevens. "The report shows she entered the room, and the video as well concluded that 20 seconds later, she screamed after discovering the body, correct?"

Stevens responded. "Yeah, that gives them plenty of time to stash the necklace if they were in cahoots."

Rex slowly walked to the door, the display, and then to the body. He counted as he moved. It took 15 seconds with a solid pause at the displays. "OK, assuming the necklace was out in the first place, she could have easily put it on, concealing it if she was calm." He ran through Winnipeg's entrance in his mind. "But then, not questioning right now why she'd kill him, how did she kill him that quickly?"

"Well, yeah, sure. I was just thinking out loud." In an irritated voice, he said, "Bradley, did you pull up the video of her leaving the room?"

Without answering, she placed the computer on the desk, stepping back. The video played out, showing nothing substantial. She was wearing a tight-fitting dress that possibly would have revealed whether she had worn the necklace around her neck, and she wasn't carrying anything in which she could've concealed it.

Rex looked at her. "Litimer as well?"

"Knew you were going to ask." She clicked two buttons. "Here you go."

Onscreen, the butler, dodging uniformed officers, wheeled out a cloth-covered service tray two hours after the murder took place. His face was clenched like he was walking through a minefield.

Stevens spoke in a loud voice. "He snuck the necklace out under there! This was the plan all along."

Rex almost felt sorry for him. From the moment Rex entered the room, it was obvious to him that this was the only way anything could've been concealed easily. He knew the necklace had to be in what he now knew to be a doll placed there by Gavin. Now it was just a question of who killed the security guard. "I need a few minutes alone to think this through."

Rex walked over to Penny. Quietly, he said, "Can you please get Charles on the phone?"

Penny nodded as she pulled her phone from her purse.

Stevens opened his mouth to say something and then clamped his teeth hard, holding in the words. He walked out of the room, nodding to Bradley.

Rex took the phone and walked to the corner. A second later, as quietly as he could, he said to Charles, "Hey, I need you to get one of the guys to track down an address and get over there right away."

"Can't you get it from Stevens's group?"

"Don't want to tip my hand just yet."

"Got it. What do you have?"

"Right now, just a strong hypothesis. Get an address for Calvin Litimer."

"Who's he?"

"The butler."

Almost laughing, Charles said, "Did he *do it*?"

"Just get someone competent over there, fast. When they're outside, have them call me. Don't let them enter or approach the place. Right now, just observe from a very safe distance until I figure a few things out."

"All right. How's it going with Hitch the Bitch?"

Rex grunted loudly. "As good as can be expected. You'd be proud of me. I've been a perfect gentleman."

"Usually are."

Rex hung up.

"Penny. What did you find on Helen Jackson?"

"From Facebook, she's wealthy and quite privileged. Her dad owns a chain of car dealerships."

"Not the type to nab jewels then?"

"Exactly."

"Yeah, that type's got some character flaws, but being a burglar ain't one of them."

"Unfortunately, I know the type too well. I spent most of my time at Northwestern with them. I'm telling you, she has this job to brag to her friends that she hangs with Chicago's elite. She's not working for the money."

"Sounds about right." Rex bent just in front of the coffee service tray and closed one eye, looking toward the safe. The sightline was as he expected. Turning, he watched as Penny pulled her hair behind her ear, bending, trying to see what he was looking at.

She leaned back, giving him space. "How'd you know that the ruby was a fake?"

"I didn't, but I did know that something valuable had to have been taken from the room, though. So, it was an easy enough guess when it was obvious none of the collectables had been swiped."

"How?"

"There's no other explanation, so it had to be the answer."

"Oh yeah, that's perfectly clear...as mud."

His brain was in hyperdrive. Rex knew Penny

was talking and could recite back what she was saying a month from now verbatim, but the words weren't clear right now. He walked to the desk and sat on the edge. His eyes glazed over.

The mayor and his oversized escort entered the room. He hooked a thumb at Rex and asked Penny. "Is he all right?"

Rex's eyes were wide open, and he made fists pushing them together at chest level. His focus was so great that despite his surroundings, the only thing that currently existed was the case running through his mind.

Penny responded, "He will be when he comes out of his trance and solves this case for you."

INVESTIGATION
HOUR THREE AND
TWENTY MINUTES

Rex sat with Penny in a room down the hall that held two equally sized desks. It took some effort, but he convinced Stevens to let him interview Litimer alone. The door opened, and a slender cop brought the butler in, holding his arm. Rex nodded and said, "Thank you. Please close the door when you leave."

The cop glared as he turned and followed his order. The butler's dark eyes scanned the room before settling on Rex. He looked haggard, not the way a tired person would look, but more like someone whose patience had been pushed long past endurance.

Rex, leaning on the desk, said, "Please sit." He gestured to a leather chair near him.

The man, saying nothing, continued standing.

"If you prefer to stand, that's fine. You'll see this'll go much faster if you answer my questions as quickly and as concisely as possible, sir, but it might be a while, so it might be sensible to make yourself comfortable."

"Are you more police?" He looked Rex up and down, apparently searching for a badge indicating rank. "How many times must I answer the same questions?" The man sat down slowly, wringing his hands once he was settled. He was approaching 40, yet didn't have a visible line on his face. There was a slight accent that was well-concealed, and if you weren't looking for it, it wouldn't be easy to detect.

"No. We're here as consultants to the police. You don't have to answer any of my questions, but it would be in your best interest to do so."

"Why do they need you?"

"You'd have to ask them that."

"What if, I'm not....exactly comfortable answering your questions?"

"I respect that, but would ask that you at least hear them before making that judgment." Rex then smiled, adding, "Fair enough?"

"Well, I guess I can see no harm in listening."

"Very well then." He sped up his cadence. "How long have you worked here?"

"In this house? Precisely eight years. Before that, I worked for the Hitches in their suburban home for two."

"Long time to work for someone. I'd guess that after that long, you became part of the family, in a way." The man looked past Rex to the wall behind him, purposefully not making eye contact. Rex studied the edge of the man's lip. It was curled slightly downward. "When you were in the office this morning, did you notice anything unusual in the room?"

"As I told the police earlier, no. I laid out the dishes and left the same as any other day."

His right eyebrow rose, and his hand shook slightly as his dancing lip performance continued. Rex pressed on: "You specifically asked to work today even though it was your day off, correct?"

"I'm not comfortable answering that question."

Ignoring him, Rex continued. "With all this going on, I find it curious that you'd want to be here."

"I wish I could be of more help to you, but as you said, I don't have to answer any questions. If you'll excuse me, I'll be leaving now."

He began to stand. Rex already prepped Penny on the program. It was earlier than Rex wanted, but he pounced. "Penny here is a lawyer. We can make this conversation privileged, if you'd find that easier to give us the answers we need to help you out of the jam you're in." The man's eyes pierced through Rex.

"What *exactly* are you referring to?" His Adam's apple bobbled.

"We know how you got the necklace out. What I need to know is where you're going to exchange it."

The butler's complexion left, making him appear as if someone had pulled the life out of him. He slumped back into the chair. "Sir, I have no idea what you're talking about."

The accent strengthened, showing heavily on the vowels to a trained ear. "Litimer, was it Gavin who forced you into this?"

"No! You must believe me—I didn't kill that man! I wasn't even on the same floor when the murder took place."

"I know. Mr. Litimer, what arrangements have been made to return the necklace to Gavin's associate?"

"Who told you these things?"

"That's not relevant. What is, is whether they're accurate." Studying his face, Rex knew he had him.

"I—I can't discuss this! You don't understand."

"I might more than you think. I have very skilled detectives outside your home right now."

The butler gripped the sides of his chair, leaning forward. "What! No! You have no right! Do you know what they will—"

The man stopped, grasping his mouth to try to hold the words in. It was obvious he wasn't accustomed to talking back to someone he viewed as superior. The desperation in his eyes confirmed Rex's hunch.

"Yes, I'm aware that your family is at risk. It's why we're having this conversation privately, because if the cops hear this, it will get messy quick. I need to know the exact details of how you're supposed to return the necklace to them. This is hard for you—believe me, I get it. Please understand I can help you, but I need answers—now."

"How do you...No, I won't say anymore. You say you aren't a police officer, but how am I to know that?" His eyes drifted to Penny and then quickly back to Rex. "You're a clever man."

"Look, you need to think this through carefully. I'm not going to pressure you, but right now, you have to understand that I'm the best chance you've got to get your family through this safely. The dead man's associate is getting nervous right now with each passing second and has no way of reaching you. How long do you think he'll wait before he cuts his losses? Then will he leave witnesses behind?"

"Please don't say these things!" He placed his hands over his ears as his eyes glistened. "I have a wife and daughter. They're my world. Nothing can happen to them!"

"Mr. Litimer, the police know you took the necklace from the room. They're going to work you over, and it will take several hours. The clock's already ticking here for you to get back to the man holding your family hostage."

Rex paused, letting the words sink in. Outside the door, he heard footsteps, reminding him that at any moment, Stevens could end this. "How do you think this would go as time ticks by?" Rex could see that he was close to getting through. It hurt to push someone so vulnerable, yet he pressed on. "You seem like a nice man, so I hope everything works out for you. I really do, but in my professional opinion, you're up against it. Far more than you realize. Besides everything we just discussed, at any minute, a reporter can figure out what's going on in here, and it will be all over the news. When the kidnapper sees that, it will create panic."

His eyes filled with tears. "If I tell you everything I know, what will you do to help me?"

Rex looked at Penny. "First, we'll have to get the necklace out of here safely, if it isn't already. The second part of that's just a little more complex."

INVESTIGATION HOUR
THREE AND FORTY MINUTES

Everyone was riled up just enough that Rex, for the first time, thought that his plan might work as long as Penny did her part. He put the bottle of bourbon he swiped from the mayor's bar to his lips, and it took all the strength he had not to let it go down his throat.

Stevens loudly said, "I knew you were deep into the bottle, but didn't know it was this bad, Haining."

"It ain't bad, pal. I just found that a nip here or there takes the edge off. Let's not pretend you've never had one or two on the job."

"In the mayor's office on a high-profile murder case?"

"There wasn't a murder here."

Stevens's face went slack. "Get off it, man. How drunk are you?"

"Enough." He pretended to take another slug before continuing. "But that doesn't change the fact that Gavin wasn't murdered." He glanced at his watch. If all went well, Penny should be entering the room any minute.

"You're certifiable, buddy."

Rex playfully shrugged. "Don't mean I'm

wrong."

"All right, you're going to leave now. If the mayor sees you on the way out, do us both a favor and tell him you're stumped."

Rex grabbed the bottle. "Think I'll finish up with this first, if ya don't mind."

"Don't think I won't have you escorted out, Haining."

Rex whispered under his breath, "Come on, Penny." There was a knock, and she entered as if she had heard him. He raised his eyebrows in a questioning gesture. Penny winked and pointed to her purse. Indignant, Rex shouted, "All right, all right. I'll go already."

Penny asked, "What's going on?"

Stevens responded. "Your wonder boy over here decided to get into the liquor cabinet."

"Come on!" Penny closed her eyes and sighed deeply.

Rex was very proud of her performance and slightly ashamed that he had given her so much practice being disappointed in him. He said in his best drunken slur, "I had a small taste. No biggie. I can still work."

Penny stepped across the desk, grabbing him by the arm. "I'm sure you can, but I think it's best if we go now." Fumbling in her purse, she turned her back to Stevens.

Rex pretended to stumble as he quickly took the necklace from her and shoved it down his pants. "On second thought. Don't think so. Ain't going to let these clowns bitch this case up any more than they already have."

"All right, you're out of here." In a forceful voice, Stevens bellowed into the hall. "Brenner, get in here!"

Rex whispered to Penny, "Here goes nothing." He bent forward, making sure the jewels weren't visible through his pant leg, somewhat confident he brought his attention back to them. He watched Penny's chest rise and fall much too fast. Quietly, he added, "Hey, stick to the script, and you'll be fine."

A man who looked like he had spent most of his waking hours in the gym entered the small space. Stevens pointed at Rex. "Escort Haining out of here. He's slippery, so be careful." Pulling his phone out of his jacket pocket, he added, "He gives you any trouble whatsoever, use as much force as necessary."

Rex gave a fake laugh and then said, "You'll never figure this one out without me."

"We'll see about that. Brenner, take him out the back entrance and make sure you watch him get into a cab." He placed his phone against his ear as he walked away.

"Yes, sir."

Rex said to Penny, "This was getting dull, anyway." He glanced down at his crotch. The bottom of the shirt was concealing the necklace well enough. "After you?" He walked behind Penny. When they were in front of Brenner, he gripped Rex's arm hard enough that he would've belted him in any other circumstance. He knew that if they searched him, as was procedure now that the police were aware that a priceless necklace was missing before he left, they were sunk. Knowing that distracting them was his only chance, Rex spoke louder than necessary. "What precinct you with?"

The large man silently pushed Rex through the doorway, chomping away at something with his muscular jaw.

Looking back, Rex quipped. "You're a real talker, huh?"

"Look, I want to make this as easy as it can be, so how about you play nice?" They took the stairs briskly. "I've heard stories about you through the years, and I have a lot of respect for all you've done, but don't think for a second that I won't lay you out if you make me. Understand?"

"Understood." They were at the landing leading to the second floor. Passing a cop who was nearly asleep, Rex said, "So, how long have you been on the force? You look a little long in the tooth to still be wearing your blues." His comment made the man increase his tight grip. Rex fought the urge to pull away, not wanting to give him the satisfaction. After going through a labyrinth of dark hallways, they arrived at what was once a servants' entrance, with a wall of cabinets and a bench beneath. Two cops stood at the door.

Brenner spun Rex around. He knew the frisk was coming. Rex stepped in so their faces were inches apart. "You still want to, what did you say, lay me out? How about we step outside and see what you got?"

Brenner stepped in close enough that Rex could smell the spearmint gum he had been chomping. "I wouldn't disgrace the badge in that way."

Rex balled a fist, pissed that the one guy who was chosen to escort him out was a Boy Scout when he was surrounded by cops who hated his guts and would relish a free shot at him. "Oh, you're saying I'm a disgrace?" Rex reached his hand back. Penny, picking up on his cue, stepped between them and shoved Rex. Dramatically, he went through the open door. Intentionally stumbling down the two small brick steps, he waved his arms and screamed, "Yeah, you're lucky she did that!" The cold rain coated his back, making his shirt stick to him. He glanced at the street, knowing that if Penny didn't play her part perfectly, he might have to make a run for it.

Penny stood in front of the open doorway, stopping the advancing cop. As Brenner stepped up to her, she turned, impeding his progress. She said, "I apologize for all this. We really thought he was doing better."

"Miss, I got to frisk Haining and you."

"Why me?"

"Because I'm going to have to ask you to leave as well."

"I can't just yet."

"Yeah, and why's that?"

"I'm here officially now as Mr. Litimer's lawyer and need to ask him some more questions."

"Ah, just like that, huh? Miss, come on. Let's get this over with. You know you ain't got no right to be with him until he's charged."

"Technically, you're right. Just like technically, only Rex signed the disclosure agreement. So, I can go across the street and wait with the reporters and gauge their level of interest in what I know, or we can get past these...technicalities, and we can head back upstairs?"

"This is just great!" He chomped at his gum with his eyes bulging as if they were going to pop out of his head. "You know"—his muscular arm raised as his hand went to his crew cut—"this is well above my pay grade."

"Well, I guess we'd better head upstairs then."

Looking her up and down, he finally grunted, "Come on."

In the dim light, the look of relief on her face took away some of the guilt for getting her caught up in his performance. Rex finally relaxed when the officer standing at the door yanked it shut. Feeling the cold rain, the moment of relief quickly passed, as he knew this was the easy part of what he was about to attempt to pull off.

INVESTIGATION HOUR FOUR

Rex sat patiently next to Charles in the lawyer's BMW. They were just down the street from a two-flat that looked like it hadn't been painted since the Chicago World's Fair. Also nearby was the Litimer family home. Charles was finishing a call with the mayor.

"Yes, sir. Like I said, I apologize. Rex has been struggling with his drinking, but has been clean for some time now. Believe me, I would've never sent him there if I thought for even a second—" Charles pulled the phone from his ear, rolling his eyes.

He then nodded. "Uh huh, uh huh, yeah, I wish you well with the investigation." He hit the end button and turned to Rex. "You couldn't have found a better way to get out of there? I don't like the guy, but he comes in handy for the firm from time to time."

"Maybe, but the way I look at it, we're here with the necklace. That was my priority."

Rex sized up the street, knowing that the odds of this working were slim at best. From Charles's report, the lawyer chose to stake out Litimer's house himself. Rex learned that there were front and back doors, but no basement, limiting the surveillance. The shades were drawn in the front, and the only window in the back was on the service door, which had a closed metal shutter. No matter what line they took, it was going to be tricky, and if Litimer's family were in there, they'd need to move fast as soon as the plan began.

"Charles, are you sure you're up to covering the front door?" Rex grabbed the gun from the glove compartment. It had been a long time since he last held one, yet it felt familiar.

"I got it."

Rex glanced at his former partner's growing belly. Stress from defending those who needed it most and sitting behind a desk was taking its toll on the ex-cop. "You sure, man?"

Charles nodded.

Mutual respect had been earned decades ago, yet at times like these, it grew. Charles was born into money —enough that he never had to work a day in his life —but he never acted like it. Against his father's objections, he joined the police force out of a sense of duty that many only pretended to have. When he began to realize how minimal an impact he had as a detective, he went to night school and earned a law degree, taking on mostly pro bono cases. Knowing that his only true friend was willing to still be out on the street like this because it was the right thing to do brought a tingling of pride.

Checking the clip, Rex said, "All right. Keep to the north side of the alley across the way; you should have a clear view from there."

"Understood."

Rex had run through the plan so many times that his head ached. He handed the gun to Charles and took the second one out of the glove compartment. Using Charles's phone, he texted Penny.

Can he make the call?

After nearly a minute, her response popped up.

Not yet. DA's still all over us.

Did they get him to spill anything?

Not even close. He's doing well at playing dumb.

When do you think you can get him alone?

He stared at the blinking icon, trying to will a response as the tension was settling into his neck. This was taking too long. He could feel it deep inside.

Charles asked, "What's going on?"

"She can't get him away."

Charles nervously gripped the steering wheel.

Rex could feel his friend's doubt even though he knew Charles would never speak out. He always trusted Rex's judgment, even at times when he shouldn't. It was one of his most endearing qualities. Rex's leg started bouncing up and down, shaking the phone. He stared toward the house and saw a dog that looked like it needed a meal, look both ways before crossing the street. Staring at the potholes and trash, Rex didn't envy anybody who lived on this side of the expressway. Just as he was about to type again, the phone dinged.

All right, I got them out of here. I'm going to have him call right now.

Patch me in right away, all right?

Did you think I forgot? Hang tight.

Ten seconds later, the phone rang. Rex muted the line and put it on speaker, placing it between them. A tense voice pierced the silence.

"This is Litimer. I was told to call this number."

"What's going on over there? I've been waiting for hours!" The man's voice had a thick accent.

"It was unavoidable. There's far more security than you or Mr. Gavin anticipated."

"Do you have it?"

"Is my family safe?"

"Don't question me! I gave you my word I wouldn't harm them as long as you did what you were told. Did you?"

Rex could sense the violence in the man's harsh voice. He had been around far too many who could kill without a second's hesitation. There was no doubt this man would fall within that group. Listening, hoping the butler could stick to the program, Rex made a fist trying to keep calm. It was a lot to ask of someone whose family was in peril to trust in him.

"Yes!"

"You have the ruby?"

"It's out of the mansion—and near you."

"What does that mean?"

"I couldn't get away, so I sent it with someone I trust."

"That wasn't the plan!"

"There are too many people, so I did what I had to. Listen, do you want the necklace or not?"

The unwavering delivery surprised Rex. He stared at the phone, waiting for the answer that was going to determine the fate of Litimer's family.

"Don't speak to me in this way unless you want to hear your child's last scream."

"I apologize." His voice broke on the final word. "All I want is to be done with...this... nightmare. Tell me what to do, and it shall be done."

"Who's this person that you have trusted with your family's life?"

"He's worked with me for some time at the mansion. He's like a brother to me. As you instructed, I can have him meet you in the park near my house."

"No. Have him come to the house."

Rex breathed a sigh of relief. The likelihood that he was working alone just went way up.

"Very well. He can be there within a few minutes."

"Litimer, I'll warn you one last time. I'm not a man to be trifled with. What I was sent here to do is greater than oneself. If you're trying to deceive me, I'll happily sacrifice myself after taking care of your family first."

Rex gritted his teeth.

"I understand. Please believe me. I assure you that all I want is my family back safely."

Charles nudged Rex, pointing to the front door of the house. Behind the drape, a shadow formed.

"How soon can he be here?"

"A few minutes."

"Tell your man to come to the back door." The line went silent as the shadow disappeared.

To ensure the line was clear, he hung up and redialed. "Penny?"

"Yes?"

"How's Litimer?"

"Shaken."

"Understandable. Sit tight. This will be over soon." In his mind, he added, *I hope*. Rex swallowed the doubt that he should call in official reinforcements. Arguing with himself that they could do far more harm than good, he said, "I have nothing substantial to go on, but I think there's only one man in there. That's why he changed the point of exchange."

"I had the same thought." He shifted, his belly hitting the steering wheel. "Along with the thought that once he has the jewels, he'll take out anyone in his way."

"Yeah. That's why I'm going to have to get real close when I hand them over before he blows me full of holes." Rex's eyes were glued to the building as he tried to come up with an alternate plan. "His suspicion will give me the chance." Knowing he was going to be frisked, he handed Charles the gun.

"All right, understood."

Charles finger-tapped the side of his gun near the safety. The nervous tic always came. Rex said, "I thought we were retired from this type of work."

Charles let out a deep laugh. "Hey, at least you're still in shape to handle it."

Rex instantly thought of his own sore knees and the start of love handles. "I'll be catching up to you soon enough, buddy. Charles, it's not too late to back out. Think of Trish and the kids."

"I got you into this. I'll be backing you up, like always. Besides, I know we'll get through this."

"How's that?"

"Because we always do."

Rex patted his friend's shoulder as he said, "Well, here goes nothing. Give me a full minute before you follow." He grabbed the spare phone that Charles had brought along and shoved it into his pocket.

"All right." Charles cocked the slide on the gun before pushing it into his waistband.

The familiar sound stirred memories Rex wished he had more distance from. In seconds, he was out of the car and dashed across the street. The rain had dissipated into a mist that barely wet him. Hiding in the shadows outside the streetlamp's light, a familiar calmness came over him, as it always had. It was like his brain and nervous system had a cruise control button that he didn't have access to until it was an absolute necessity. Whenever he had to be sharp, it kicked in, bringing a brief reprieve from the tension that would surface when he was alone, viciously driving him to drink away the anxiety.

JASON FISCHER

The El train in the distance rattled, echoing into the night, and the rotting garbage from the dumpster he had just passed by made his lunch turn in his stomach. Rex closed his right eye as he made his way to the house. The trick had served him well as cheap night vision, in case he was about to enter a pitch-black house. Jumping over a small puddle in the alleyway, his open eye was like a camera lens, taking in every trace and curve of the brick buildings surrounding him. Crossing a lawn that was mainly dirt, with pathetic clumps of weeds, he was ready for the door to fling open and a gun to mow him down. The man would be insane to kill without so much as seeing the necklace first, yet the image stuck there. He ascended the worn concrete steps slowly, straining to hear anything from inside the closed door.

Before he could knock, it swung open, revealing a bearded man who looked like he hadn't slept in a week, holding a Smith & Wesson. The fact that he wasn't wearing a mask set off an alarm somewhere deep inside Rex, in a place that had been dormant for some time.

"Get in here." The man waved the gun as his eyes scanned the alley.

There was little light behind him. Rex brought his hands shoulder high and slowly stepped forward, staring at the man's finger, which was wrapped tightly around the trigger. Before Rex entered, he said as weakly as he could muster, "I need to see my friend's family first." Rex made his hands shake and bowed his head, playing the part to perfection. "I'm sorry."

"Get in here!"

Rex leaned back, going down the steps. Seeing there was no silencer on the pistol made his confidence grow that the abductor wouldn't pull the trigger out in the open. "Please, please don't hurt me!"

The man stood as if an invisible barrier prevented him from leaving the house. "Show me the ruby. Now!"

Rex, chancing it, pulled it from under his shirt. He had been wearing it around his neck. "I'm sorry, but he made me promise to see his family before I turn it over."

The man's unibrow tensed. "Get in here. Now!"

Rex took a step forward. Baiting him.

The man, with his free hand, leaned forward, reaching for the ruby. Rex didn't think when the barrel lowered and went slightly to the right. He quickly grabbed the man's forearm, pulling him into his knee as Rex pushed the gun to the side. The blow landed squarely in the upper abdomen, just beneath the ribcage.

After the man didn't even flinch, Rex knew he was dealing with ex-military. He spun and pulled Rex's arm over his shoulder. As he bent to flip him, Rex, with his free arm, jabbed the man's kidney with enough force that Rex hoped he wouldn't be able to continue. As the man went to the ground, Rex kicked him squarely in the back and, with a solid twist, freed the gun from his hand. Kneeling on top of him, he jammed the gun into the man's ear hard enough that it made a thudding noise.

"Where are the Litimers?" The man stunk of spent adrenaline and body odor. Rex's eyes were focused forward, waiting for the man's cavalry to come rushing in.

The man, breathing heavily, whispered something in another language.

Knowing time wasn't his friend, Rex leaned into the gun, mashing the tender flesh around the man's ear. "If I have to ask again, I'll shoot this ear off first before I shoot your kneecap." He twisted the point of the metal deep into the lobe, drawing blood. "So, do we understand each other?"

In a hoarse tone, the man spat out, "Tied up… two rooms down."

"Are they alone?"

"Yes."

"Like you'd tell me if they weren't." Rex jerked the man up from the ground, using him as a shield. "Take me to them now." The man grasped at his side and was wheezing so loudly it sounded like whistling. Rex kept him tight against him, not wanting to give him room for any leverage. The hallway ahead was narrow and dark. Peeking over the man's shoulder, Rex held his breath, trying to hear anything that would expose a potential threat. Pushing the large bulk in front of him, they entered the darkness. The man reached for a light switch.

Rex leaned in, hissing, "Leave it."

There was a thud and a sharp cry ahead. He knew he should call for backup, but didn't feel confident that if the man wasn't alone, the second kidnapper wouldn't do something drastic. Rex spun the large man around, pinning him against the wall, then said quietly, "Where are they—in there?" He shoved the gun deep into the man's neck. The flash in his eye told Rex what he didn't say. Rex was acclimating to the darkness, but not enough that he was sure there wasn't someone down the hall. He pulled the man along until they were directly across from what he assumed was a bedroom door. Glancing down at the hardwood floor, he saw a small glimmer of light.

Pressing forward a few inches, Rex screamed, "Mrs. Litimer?" There was a grunt. Rex would bet his life that it had come from the door to his right. Shoving the man against the wall, Rex pivoted, leaned against him, and kicked the door open. There was a single dim light in a tiny bedroom. A gagged middle-aged woman was fighting against a rope securing her to a chair, moaning and pointing with her eyes to the floor. A little girl was on the hardwood floor in front of her, not moving. The child's color was off, way off. Rex turned and nailed the man at the base of the neck. He went down with a solid thud.

Rex entered the room, clearing the space behind the door, and kicked open the closet door, revealing only clothing and board games. The adrenaline coursed through him, making his hands cold. It felt familiar and somehow comforting. Aiming the gun as he kneeled at the door, he stood in front of the woman and pulled the phone from his pocket. Suddenly, everything was going in slow motion as he stared at the open doorway.

Charles's voice came through. "You in?"

"Get in here now; use the front door. Go slow. I think we're alone, except for the man you'll see lying in the hall, but I don't know for sure."

"Be there in a hot second."

Rex felt for the girl's pulse on her neck. Her skin was cold. He paused his breath, needing quiet. The woman behind him moaned. Over his shoulder, he hissed, "Ma'am, everything's going to be all right. I need you to be quiet for a minute, though. Please." Between his own heartbeats, he listened for anyone approaching, his eyes narrowed to slits, focused on the hall.

He pressed harder against the girl's cool flesh, not getting anything. His eyes were still trained on the hallway when he heard what he hoped was his partner busting in. "Charles, back here, two doors to your left."

"Coming."

He was never so happy to hear his friend's voice. Rex knew they weren't out of the woods yet. There was the sound of a door kicking in next to them and then shuffling across a hardwood floor. The second he saw Charles fill the doorway, he took a deep breath for the first time since he entered the house.

Charles was holding his gun steady. Rex put his own down, saying, "Did you clear the other bedroom?"

"Yeah."

As he walked into the room, Rex called out, "Get an ambulance here." He then began CPR.

INVESTIGATION HOUR FIVE

Rex sat at a desk that he never thought he'd see again, glaring at Mayor Hitch. He was sitting in his custom-made red leather chair. Charles had just finished calming him down enough that the red in his cheeks was almost gone.

Hitch sighed before saying, "Although I appreciate that you have returned the ruby and apparently apprehended a man who was holding my employee's family hostage, I still need to know who killed the man lying in the office just across that hall!"

Penny was sitting between Rex and Charles. Her forehead was bunched. It was a telltale sign that the stress was getting to her. Moments like this reminded him of how young she still was. Rex spoke for the first time since they entered the room a few minutes ago. Glancing at the paper in front of the mayor, he said, "I'll explain everything if you promise not to hold Mr. Litimer or me accountable for any of our actions this evening."

"As I explained to his...counsel," the mayor paused, glaring at Penny as though she were something he had found under his shoe, "while you were making your way over here, I'll make no such deal. I've been cooperative enough to let him go visit his wife and, fortunately, recovering child at the hospital, but that's as far as I'll go."

"Well then, I guess we're at an impasse, Mayor."

"Like hell, we are, Haining! You're not going to withhold evidence and walk out of here scot-free."

"What evidence am I withholding? You have the ruby."

"You know damn well what I'm talking about. You know who killed that man, and you're going to tell me."

"What I have is a hypothesis that cannot be substantiated without the cooperation of your office. I need no justification not to share it. My ideas can neither be proved nor disproved; therefore, I have no legal or ethical responsibility to share it and won't unless we can come to an agreement."

The mayor leaned back, working over the bottom of his jaw. His Harvard alumni ring glistened in the light. Rex rarely liked anyone from the Ivy League crowd because most didn't earn the status that gave them a leg up on everyone else who had to fight and claw for a better place in this world.

Charles spoke calmly, as he usually did. "Hitch, I understand your position and hope that you trust me enough to understand that I'm—excuse me, *we're*—not playing hardball here to force you into something you wouldn't logically agree to on your own."

Rex bit his tongue to keep from yelling, "*I am.*" The anxiety that had plagued him since he was a child was creeping into his bones, making it hard to hold everything in.

Charles continued with his best, well-rehearsed understanding expression. "This is all going to open up to the press and blow up. We're just trying to protect our client's best interests here. I'll give you my word that this can all be resolved and that you'll come out shining in the best light. That's why I'm asking you for your cooperation."

"You're asking for a lot of trust, considering Haining already slipped away from the crime scene." Hitch chewed his lower lip before continuing. "Beyond that, your assistant has threatened to go to the press, which is a pretty underhanded move. Now, you're asking me to trust you?"

Charles responded instantly. "Yes. Rex, for the record, didn't slip away. Your police force physically removed him. Penny never explicitly said she was going to talk to the press; she merely stated that if she were forced away from her client, she'd be questioned by them, and it would be within her legal right to speak with them. Look, until now, everything we've done has been in our client's best interests. You can't blame us for that, and you must realize that we won't share privileged information given to us in confidence without protection. This is the simplest solution that will gain the most for both parties involved."

"Charles, I know I don't have to ask this, as you aren't the type to defend someone who's guilty. However, can you assure me that Litimer had nothing at all to do with the murder?"

Rex sat up straight. "I can do you one better. Like I already told your lead investigator, there was no murder."

Hitch looked at Charles and said, "And you expect me to believe this nonsense?"

Charles glanced at Rex before he said unconvincingly, "As stated...yes, sir."

Stevens, for the first time since they locked themselves in the room, said, "Sir, you're not really considering this, are you?" He was standing next to a statue of a dog that looked like it ate steroids at every meal.

Hitch quieted him down with a single stare. The tall man's chest rose as he bit back his next comment. Rex wasn't proud of it, but he felt the beginnings of a smile curl at the edge of his lip.

The mayor pulled a large gold-plated pen from its perch on his massive desk and scribbled on the paper Penny had drafted. He placed the pen on the desk and lightly flicked it, watching it roll away. Coming out of his trance, he looked up and, in a resigned voice, said, "All right, I guess I asked for it after the way we parted last time, Haining. Because I trust Charles not to pull a fast one, I signed your paper. Now, would you please tell me what happened?"

Rex closed his eyes for a brief instant to gather his thoughts. He promised Charles that if they got their way, he wouldn't take any shots at the mayor. He considered asking Stevens to be removed, which would have made it easier to keep the promise. Instead, while making small circles with his finger on his leg, he said, "The deceased orchestrated everything that took place this evening."

Stevens took a step forward, as he nearly shouted. "Oh, here we go!"

"Do you mind quieting him down?" Rex stared daggers at the man he felt should've been removed from the force years ago.

The mayor quietly said, "Unless they're direct questions, Stevens, please keep your comments to yourself."

Rex didn't hesitate. "Have you recovered the missing doll?" Rex knew the answer, but was covering his tracks. After he got back from Litimer's house, he had Penny sneak into the pantry and replace the ruby before Charles called in an anonymous tip as to the doll's location.

"Yes", Stevens replied.

"Let me guess—the doll was hollow and had a camera and the authentic ruby?"

"Yes, but no murder weapon."

"We'll get to that."

"Don't need you to. Litimer will eventually talk and tell us where he hid it." His face was a web of wrinkles, calculating.

"No, I'm certain you won't." Rex shifted in his chair as the thunder outside roared. The rain had picked up again as soon as he got back to the mansion. "The tiny camera lens was there so that Gavin could get the combination. You see, it was essential for his plan to work that only a murder took place in that room and not a robbery, or else he could have forcefully gotten into the safe."

"But you just said there was no murder!" Stevens yelled.

"I said appeared, not that it actually did. Please, this will go much faster if you stop interrupting." Stevens opened his lips, then stopped. "You see, from the beginning, that was the goal of Gavin: To replace the ruby and get it out of here, undetected. When the visit was first planned months ago, he and the security team were able to view pictures of the room. With a little research, he found what he was looking for: an item that was hollow that could conceal not only the camera, but also the fake jewels."

Rex kept speaking, moving his hand to the armrest. His finger moved so quickly it made a noise as it traced the leather armchair. "He could have swapped it and waited until sun-up in Sri Lanka and taken the chance that when his boss put it back on, in Gavin's presence, nobody would notice it was fake. From what I've read, there's a rather elaborate ritual when it's taken off and then put back on, and anyone who was so accustomed to it would have had a good chance of noticing the switch. If that had happened, the room would've been searched on the spot, and Gavin would've been sunk. So, I assume that he devised a foolproof plan to sneak the original out."

Rex paused and took a sip of ice-cold water

with lemon. The ice against his lip elicited a craving he was afraid he'd be giving in to very soon. "So, how'd he do that? Perhaps create a diversion of a locked-room mystery that would allow someone who was being forced to cooperate a chance to remove the doll unnoticed, which the video confirmed when the refreshment cart was wheeled out."

"So, you're saying your man Litimer was that person? And then along the way had the thought of knocking off Gavin and keeping the loot for himself?"

Rex ignored Stevens's outburst and swiped the papers off the desk as the mayor leaned forward to grab them. "Please, everyone! Remember, this is a working hypothesis. Let me get everything out before jumping to conclusions."

Penny took the papers from Rex and, folding them, put them on her lap.

Hitch pointed at Charles. "If this is going where I think it is—"

Charles interrupted. "Jacob, please, you know me better than that."

Rex, no longer caring about his promise to Charles, blurted out, "So, let's work through that. Litimer killed Gavin to exchange a necklace that nobody could fence. To be clear, that's your theory, right, Stevens?"

"Yeah. The more you talk, the more I like it."

Rex continued, "How did he get in the room? Was he inside the doll, next to your magical gun, knife, or whatever that left no apparent trace? Think, man!"

"All right, strike that!" He looked down shamefully. "It's been a long day!" Jerking his head up, his eyes flashed. "But wait a second. If the necklace couldn't be sold, why did he take it?"

"I believe he was taking the jewels for what he thought was the greater good of his people because he believed it was time for a new president to be nominated, and whoever possessed the ruby would give them the ability to do it. He so passionately believed in his cause that he stabbed himself."

Rex eyed the room, taking in everyone's reaction. "It's the only answer. He had the combination through the recording device. Then he switched out the ruby, hiding it in the doll that he was going to have Litimer remove from the room while he himself created a distraction."

Hitch leaned forward, asking, "So he committed suicide because he believed it would help another president to be elected?"

"Yes. The M.E.'s report showed he was terminally ill, and his military record indicated he was a devoted citizen. So much so that, after serving his country, he was willing to risk his life while guarding the ruby nightly, as there had been previous attempts to steal it when the former president was in office. So, if his time was limited, I believe he was willing to take his own life to sneak the ruby out."

Hitch leaned back in his chair, letting out a

whistle.

"Back to my previous comment, I'll need your team to substantiate my hypothesis. I need you to send the lab folks back in and look for a weapon that isn't necessarily a weapon. Perhaps a pen or something on one of the dolls that he could have used to stab himself, then wipe on his own shirt to get rid of most of the blood residue. I assume that after removing the visually detectable blood from the instrument, he used the bleach wipe in his pocket to clean the rest. As we know, the blood spatter isn't perfectly consistent with the streaks on his shirt, making my theory plausible."

Rex paused, seeing that Hitch was beginning to believe him. Although he viewed the mayor as ruthless, Rex never questioned the man's intelligence. "The fact that his accomplice hasn't asked about him tells me that suicide had been the plan from the start."

Stevens nearly yelled, "And you expect me to buy this?"

"Buy what exactly, Stevens? It's the only viable solution, other than a ghost. Take a close look at the wound. My money is on the tin soldier's bayonet. It was askew in the picture of the room that we requested. I assume your techs thoroughly went through every square inch of the place. I've worked with them; they're pros. But now tell them to look for traces of bleach and for a comparison of the instrument vs. the wound."

Mayor Hitch leaned back, staring at Rex. "So,

all this, and it ends up being death, possibly by misadventure, over jewelry?"

"Seems that way until the theory is disproven with actual evidence."

The mayor shook his head, "And you thought I'd hold Litimer legally responsible for being blackmailed into the crime? Charles, you really think that's the type of man I am?"

Rex answered for him. "Considering our history, not to be offensive to someone in your... esteemed position, I figured it was in his best interest not to leave that open for interpretation."

"I'd never treat him like that!"

"Maybe not with the press around, but possibly let him go a few weeks down the road, perhaps citing another reason. Come off it, man. I know where the bodies are buried in this office." The mayor's stare personified anger. Rex clenched his fist, wondering how good it would feel to knock the look off his face. Knowing he was close to being far away from here, he said, "Look, you have everything you wanted. It's just after dinner, and you have the case neatly wrapped up. The lab folks will have confirmation soon enough. Go and do what you do best. Enjoy what's left of the party and fill your war chest. I can't and won't speak to anyone, so let's call it a night."

Stevens nearly shouted. "You think you're getting off that easy? You removed evidence from the scene."

"What evidence is that?"

"The ruby!"

Rex knew it was coming; that's why he insisted that Hitch sign the agreement that cleared both himself and Litimer. He was careful covering his tracks, but with so many cameras around, he wanted insurance. "Do you have actual proof of that?"

"I have your girl here on camera going into the pantry before you pulled your ruse to get out of here, and have her going in again after you came back. So, it's pretty obvious why she did that. There's no way you went to Litimer's house without the necklace, so that's pretty solid evidence."

Rex turned to Penny. "Why did you go into the pantry?"

"I thought it was the ladies' room."

Stevens jumped on her. "Really! Twice?"

Shrugging, she said, "Yeah, not proud of it, but this house, with all the corridors and doors, is pretty easy to get lost in."

"You, a lawyer, got lost twice? You really expect me to believe that?"

Rex said, "You really expect me to believe that a man with an army at his disposal couldn't figure out that the doll was missing in the first place?"

"You son of a bitch—you always got to antagonize, don't you. If the mayor hadn't cleared you with that agreement, I'd have you!" Stevens' chest rose and fell. "Forgetting the ruby, you still interfered with the investigation by going to Litimer's house."

"I was following a hunch and got attacked at gunpoint. That, let me remind you, happened on a case the mayor summoned me to investigate. You might want to look up the word *interfering*."

Mayor Hitch barked. "Cool it." He leaned back, steepling his fingers in front of his face. "Listen, you got what you wanted, Haining—showing us all how incompetent we are—and I can put this mess behind me without much heartburn. So, if you're willing to leave by the back entrance and honor your nondisclosure agreement, let's just go our separate ways and not dig into exactly what you or Penny did here tonight."

For the first time since he left his townhouse, his senses slowed down enough that he felt almost like himself—the self he was hopefully becoming by getting away from this type of work, not the person he used to be. It was unfamiliar just to let go, but it was beginning to feel almost right.

Thinking of the peace of his worn couch and a paperback, he looked at the mayor and said almost amicably, "Sounds like a plan, sir." As he stood up, he said to Stevens, "Hey, now that I did your job for you, do you want to personally give me a ride to the suburbs?" He winked at Penny as the harried detective taught him a fine combination of very choice expletives.

ABOUT THE AUTHOR

Jason Fischer

From a young age, Jason has always loved books. It started with an Alfred Hitchcock anthology, given to him by his uncle, Eugene Izzi, the acclaimed crime writer, and continues today with Ray Bradbury, Robert Aickman, Stephen King, and Joe Hill.

During the pandemic, he decided he wanted his own work on the bookshelves and began writing.

Early anthology successes led him to create his own short story collections and expand into the world of novels.

When he's not writing, you can find him biking the trails around his home, playing with his nephews, or on the deck, feeding the deer and enjoying nature. He is supported by his wife of 30 years, Julie. They live in the far south suburbs of Chicago.

BOOKS BY THIS AUTHOR

Your Place Is Here Now: 10 Tales Of Horror And The Supernatural

"Your place is here now." It sounds like an invitation. It's actually a command.

In this collection of horrors, Jason Fischer turns familiar spaces into deadly traps:

A dinner with a new "mother" who wasn't invited. A Halloween visitor offers a treat you must not refuse. A puzzle book that predicts your future—and takes its cut. A cardboard cutout boy that won't stay where it's put. A dark carnival ride with no power runs perfectly on what you fear most.

These and other tales of folk, psychological, and elevated horror converge on one message: your place is here now. Take your seat.

BOOKS BY THIS AUTHOR

The Haunting Of Towne Point Mall: 10 Interconnected Tales Of Terror

ATTENTION SHOPPERS: EVERYTHING MUST GO.

The grand opening of Towne Point Mall is here! Join us for:

- A very special Halloween clearance event (now featuring skeleton children)
- New clothing arrivals daily (our elves are dying to assist you)
- Professional juggling demonstrations (watch your loved ones disappear from memory!)
- Video arcade specials (where your high score could cost your soul)
- Special midnight movie screenings (these films hunger for fresh audiences)
- Luxury sleep clinic (dream with us forever... and ever... and ever...)

In these interconnected tales of retail terror, Jason Fischer transforms everyday shopping into a supernatural nightmare.

NO RAINCHECKS.
NO REFUNDS.
NO ESCAPE.

Made in the USA
Columbia, SC
17 December 2025